The Dog

by Sylvia Vanerka

Editorial Offices: Glenview, Illinois • Parsippany, New Jersey • New York, New York
Sales Offices: Boston, Massachusetts • Duluth, Georgia • Glenview, Illinois
Coppell, Texas • Sacramento, California • Mesa, Arizona

The dog has food.

The dog has water.

The dog has a home.

The dog has a bed.

The dog has toys.

The dog has a friend.

Santa's Time Off

Santa's Time Off

Poems by Santa as told to Bill Maynard

Paintings by
Tom Browning

SCHOLASTIC INC.
New York Toronto London Auckland Sydney

Perhaps you've wondered what I do when I'm not bringing toys to you....

Christmas Colors

Do you like to paint or to color or draw?
It's a great way to show someone else what you saw
You can show what you saw when you rode on your sled
You can show what you see when you stand on your head

When I paint, I forget about Christmas and toys
I don't think about presents for girls or for boys
But no matter what colors are there in the scene
Every picture I paint still turns out *red and green!*

Hop To It

A golf shot must be pretty bad
To wind up on a lily pad
And when my elves reach for my ball
They must be careful not to fall
They'd make a SPLASH that might offend
The frog who thinks he's found a friend

Fish List

You send me letters filled with lists
Or climb upon my knee
To tell me things you'd like to find
Beneath your Christmas tree
A telescope to watch the stars
A model train with lots of cars
Some Rollerblades, a top that spins
And soccer socks to guard your shins
A dinosaur that's big and green
Some snails to keep your fish tank clean
A kite to fly, a boat to sail
Some tools with wood that you can nail
A doll, a TV game to share
And several things that you can wear
A punching bag, a basketball
A poster for your bedroom wall
Some candy canes, a drum to play
A watch that tells the time of day,
A firetruck, some skates, a sled
A book like this to read in bed

To rest my mind from all this wishing
I go fishing

Horseplay

A horse is tall. A horse is wide
It's much too big for elves to ride
And if you'd *really* like to laugh
Just ask an elf to rope a calf

An elf can wear a cowboy hat
An elf can rope a cowboy's *cat*

His rope is small. His hopes are big
Perhaps someday he'll rope a pig

Could you become a *buckaroo*?
l bet you could, and I could, too
My elves would be surprised, of course
To see *me* riding on a horse

It's not that I find reindeer strange
But everybody likes a change

Hooked

With rocks and trees, and winds that gust
When casting hooks, I find I must
Be careful not to catch myself
Or, even worse, to catch an elf

To Each His Beach

I wonder if my polar bears
Would like to sit in folding chairs
To watch the surf roll up the sand
Perhaps they'd rather swim, or stand

I wonder if my caribou
Would look for rocks and shells. Would you?
It's difficult sometimes to tell
What other folks will think is swell

My elves are happy at the beach
They build their castles out of reach
Of crashing waves that soak your skin
And smash things when the tide comes in

For elves it's lots of fun, you know
To build with sand instead of snow

Crab Grab

Each barefoot elf
Has tiny toes
That lead the way
Each place he goes
Though walking barefoot's cool and nice
I always give the same advice:
Watch where you're going
Inch by inch
And stay away
From things that pinch

Rock Star

There are stars in the sky
That can help sailors steer
And a star on your tree
Means that Christmas is near

But the day I went wading
With no shoes or socks
I just wasn't expecting
A star on the rocks

Music Makers

My elves and I have formed a band
We like to think the sound is grand
But every time we play a song
I must admit: *Some notes are wrong*
And yet we play. Do you know why?
Because it's lots of fun to try!

Balancing Act

Do you remember how it feels
To ride a bike with training wheels?
And when the training wheels are gone
And you are rolling on and on
You think: Is there a chance at all
I'll learn to ride before I fall?
It's like a lot of things you plan
At first you can't, *and then you can*

At home the reindeer pull my sled
But here I have to pump instead
Yet if I never rode a bike
How would I know which bike you'd like?

Car Tune

When I'm not going far
I may tune up my car
Just to see if it goes all the way

But when toys *must* arrive
Between midnight and five
Then I tend to depend on my sleigh

Santa's Turn

We all could sing a song
Or play a game
Or read a book
BUT. . .
If anybody
Wants to eat
Somebody has to cook!

Life-Size

When I bake, I can get
Lots of help from my elves
Who insist upon cookies
As big as themselves

As for batter, I roll it
Right after I sift it
And when it's cut out
It takes *two* elves to lift it

Imagine a cookie
That's bigger than you
Do you think you could eat it?
Well, that's what elves do!

Slip Up

Whether big or *not* big, you are wise if you see
That the size that you are is the right size to be
When you skate like my elves, it is good to be small
'Cause you can't fall as far as you can if you're tall

What is it?

It's often black
It's round
It rolls
You stick
Your fingers
In the holes

When things are up
It knocks them down
And if you miss
It makes you frown

It's round
It's smooth
It's nice to see
But never
on a Christmas tree!

Downhill Spill

My elves all love to ski with me.
Regretfully, I've found
An elf who's in a snowball
Will go 'round and *'round* and *'ROUND!*

Easy Putt

For North Pole golf, where greens are white
You must equip yourself
With brightly colored golf balls
Plus a shovel and an elf

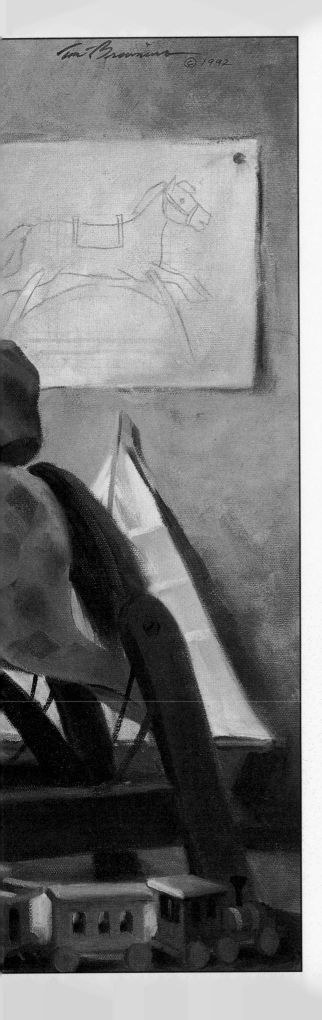

Back to Work

To enjoy your time off
There must be time *on*
So whatever I've done
And wherever I've gone
When I've sailed
And I've skied
And I've biked
And I've bowled
And I've golfed
And I've cooked
And I've fished
And I've strolled
Then it's time to head home
There are things I must do
'Cause I'd like to have Christmas *next* year
Wouldn't you?

*This book is dedicated with love
to my beautiful granddaughter, Jordan Taylor*
—TB

For Marilyn
—BM

ISBN 0-590-04939-9

Text copyright © 1997 by Bill Maynard.
Illustrations copyright © 1997 by Tom Browning.
All rights reserved. Published by Scholastic Inc.,
555 Broadway, New York, NY 10012, by arrangement
with G. P. Putnam's Sons, a division of
The Putnam & Grosset Group.

12 11 10 9 8 7 6 5 4 3 2 1   8 9/9 0 1 2 3/0

Printed in the U.S.A.   14
First Scholastic printing, November 1998

Artwork for this book is provided
courtesy of Arbor Green Publications (Sisters, Oregon).